Billie B. Brown Books

Hey Jack! Books

First American Edition 2020
Kane Miller, A Division of EDC Publishing
Original Title: Billie B Brown: The Book Buddies
Text Copyright © 2019 Sally Rippin
Illustration Copyright © 2019 Aki Fukuoka
Logo and Design Copyright © 2019 Hardie Grant Egmont
First published in Australia by Hardie Grant Egmont

All rights reserved, including the rights of reproduction
in whole or in part in any form.

For information contact:
Kane Miller, A Division of EDC Publishing
P.O. Box 470663
Tulsa, OK 74147-0663
www.kanemiller.com
www.edcpub.com
www.usbornebooksandmore.com

Library of Congress Control Number: 2019951182

Printed and bound in the United States of America
2 3 4 5 6 7 8 9 10
ISBN: 978-1-68464-135-2

The Book Buddies

By Sally Rippin

Illustrated by
Aki Fukuoka

Kane Miller

A DIVISION OF EDC PUBLISHING

Chapter One

Billie and Jack are **best friends**. They live next door to each other. In class, they sit next to each other. At recess, they play together.

Billie and Jack do *everything* together.

If Billie swings on the monkey bars, Jack swings too. If Jack wants to play soccer, Billie will play soccer too.

It's good to have a **best friend**, isn't it?

This year, Billie and Jack's class are doing a Reading Challenge. Everyone will have a book buddy. The pair that reads the most books wins.

Billie *really* wants to win. Billie finds reading easy. She reads everything!

Billie reads books,

comics, even recipes!

Jack finds reading hard.

"I don't want to be in the challenge," he tells Billie. "Reading gives me a headache!"

"Don't worry," Billie says. "I'll help you. Let's go tell Ms. Walton we want to be book buddies."

She **smiles** at Jack.

Ms. Walton *always* lets them work together.

But today, Ms. Walton has other ideas.

"Actually, Billie, your buddy is a five-year-old," Ms. Walton says. "And Jack, you will have a book buddy from grade six."

Billie's mouth drops open in shock.

Jack's legs begin to **shake**.

"But ... but ... Jack and I are best friends. We *always* work together!" Billie says.

"Every student has a book buddy from a different class," Ms. Walton explains.

"That way, you will get to know other students in the school."

"But I don't want to have a *baby* as a book buddy!" Billie says. "I'll **never** win the Reading Challenge with a five-year-old. They are **terrible** at reading."

"Sometimes there are more important things than winning, Billie," Ms. Walton says.

Then she turns around
to finish writing on the
board.

But Billie *likes* winning!

"This is the worst day
ever!" she says to Jack.
They walk out onto the
playground. Billie crosses
her arms and frowns.

Jack says nothing.

Jack feels so **nervous** that his tummy begins to ache.

Poor Billie and Jack. What will they do?

Chapter Two

The next day Billie and Jack walk to school. Billie and Jack always walk together. This morning Jack is very quiet. Billie knows something is up.

"What's wrong?" Billie asks.

Jack grumbles. "I have a tummy ache," he says.

"You're worried about the Reading Challenge, aren't you?" Billie asks.

Jack nods. "I can't have a buddy from grade six!" he says.

His tummy flips about like a fish. "I'm a terrible reader. They will get **so mad** at me!"

Billie chews her lip.

Before, Billie had only been worried about herself. But now she feels worried for Jack, too.

Some of those grade six kids are **scary!** What if he gets put with a big bully? She tries to think of something to say that will make him feel better.

"Maybe you will get a nice one?" Billie says hopefully. But she feels **nervous**.

Why won't Ms. Walton just let them be book buddies?

Billie and Jack are best friends. They do **everything** together!

When they get to class,
everyone sits down on
the mat. Ms. Walton reads
out the names of their
book buddies.

Billie sits close to Jack
and holds his hand. She
can hear him breathing
heavily. She has to think
of a way to help him.
And fast!

Suddenly Billie has an idea. A **super-duper** idea!

"Ms. Walton!" she says. "I think Jack is sick. Look how pale he is! Can I please take him to the nurse?"

Everyone looks at Jack. It's true, he is very pale.

"I don't know …"
Ms. Walton says. "His
buddy is waiting for him."

Jack coughs and puts his
hand on his tummy.

"Oh, Ms. Walton, I think he's *really* sick!" Billie says.

"All right," Ms. Walton says. She looks worried. "You can take him to the nurse, Billie. But then go straight to your buddy's classroom. Your buddy will be waiting for you, too!"

Billie grabs Jack's hand
and pulls him out of the
classroom.

"Thanks, Billie!" Jack
says. "You're the best!"

Billie sighs. "I *wish* we could work together!" she says. "I don't know why Ms. Walton won't let us be buddies. She *always* lets us work together!"

Would you like it if your teacher didn't let you work with your best friend?

Chapter Three

Billie leaves Jack in the nurse's office. She runs across the playground. Her head feels **fizzy** and **hot**. Why was she put with a baby?

Lola got Olivia Price
as her book buddy!
Olivia is in grade five.
That is SO NOT FAIR.
They will read so many
books together. They
will definitely win the
Reading Challenge.

Billie arrives at her
buddy's classroom.

"Hello!" says a teacher.
"I'm Mr. Parker. You must
be Jamila's book buddy?"

Billie nods. She tries
to smile but she is still
feeling too **cross**.

"Jamila, look who is
here!" Mr. Parker says.

Billie looks over at some
kids playing in the corner.

The smallest one looks up
from their game.

When she sees Billie,
she smiles **the biggest
smile** Billie has ever
seen.

Billie feels the **big
angry ball** in her belly
melt. Jamila is *very* cute.

"Jamila's parents don't
speak English,"
Mr. Parker tells Billie.

"That's why she needs extra help with her reading," he says.

Jamila jogs towards Billie. She has a whole pile of books in her arms.

"Hi, Jamila!" Billie says. "Show me what you're reading."

Jamila holds out a book.

Billie opens it up. The book has one word on each page and big bright pictures. She looks up at Jamila's teacher.

"Can I really count these books for the Reading Challenge?" Billie asks him. "There is only one word on each page!"

Mr. Parker smiles. "As long as you help Jamila read them," he says.

"**Wow!**" says Billie to Jamila. "We are going to read so many books together!"

Billie sits down on the cushions in the reading corner.

Jamila sits next to her
and snuggles in very
close. Billie **giggles**.
*Maybe this won't be so bad
after all?* she thinks. *And
maybe I can still win the
challenge?*

Billie opens a book and
points. "What's this word,
Jamila?" she says.

Jamila squints her eyes.

"Duh … oh … guh," she spells out slowly.

"**Yes!**" says Billie, happily. "What does that spell?"

Jamila looks up at Billie and shrugs.

"Look at the picture, Jamila," Billie says.

Billie points to the
picture of a puppy.

"Puppy?" says Jamila.

"Look at the word,
Jamila," Billie says kindly.
"It starts with 'd.'"

"**Dinosaur?**" Jamila says.

Billie sighs.

Oh dear! Learning to
read can be hard, can't it?

Chapter Four

Jack lies in the nurse's office staring at the walls. His tummy hurts and he feels scared and alone. The nurse pokes her head around the corner.

"Hey, Jack!" she says.
"There is someone here
to see you."

"Who is it?" Jack asks,
nervously.

The nurse smiles. "It's
your book buddy!" she
says.

"Oh no!" says Jack.
"What is *he* doing here?"

The nurse shrugs.
"I guess you're about to
find out!" she says.

Jack sits up in bed.
His tummy hurts really
badly now. *Why is my*
book buddy here? he
thinks. *Is he* **mad** *at me?*

Jack feels his heart jump
about like a rabbit.

He quickly slides down into the bed again. Then he pulls the sheet over his face.

Jack hears someone walk into the room. He hears them sit beside the bed.

"**Hey, Jack!**" comes a voice. "You in there somewhere?"

Jack says nothing. He thinks if he stays very still, maybe his book buddy will go away.

"My teacher sent me here to read to you," the book buddy says. "So, I have to read. Otherwise I will get into trouble. I don't care if you listen or not."

Jack lies very still.
He hears the book
buddy open a book and
turn the page.

"Chapter one," the book buddy begins. "The boy who lived."

Jack listens to his book buddy read. He listens so hard his ears hurt. Suddenly he sits up.

"That's *Harry Potter*!" he says. "I know that story. I've seen the movie."

He looks up at his big,
scary book buddy.
He has seen him on the
playground before. He is
one of the tough kids.

"Hi," the book buddy says. He sticks out his hand. "I'm Max."

Jack looks at Max's hand. "I'm Mack," Jack says. "I mean Jax!"

Sometimes when Jack is **nervous** his words get all mixed up. He squeezes his eyes shut. His cheeks burn hot.

Max chuckles. Jack opens his eyes. He sees a big grin on his book buddy's face. Suddenly he doesn't look so scary anymore.

"I do that all the time!"
Max says. "Mix up words."

"**No way!**" says Jack.
He can't believe a grade
six kid could mix up his
words. Grade six kids
know everything!

"When I was your age,
I was in the Special
Group," Max says.

"Me too!" says Jack. "*I'm* in the Special Group. To help with my reading."

Max nods. "I used to hate reading," he says.

"I hate reading, too!" says Jack. "Books are boring!"

Max laughs kindly. "I used to think that.

But my teacher said I just had to find the right book. Then, last year, I finally tried this one." He holds up his copy of *Harry Potter*. "And now I can't stop!" he says. "I've read this book six times. Do you want me to read you a little bit more?"

"Yes, please!" says Jack. He lies back down on the bed to listen. Max reads the story out loud. He reads slowly and sometimes he mixes up a word. But Jack doesn't care. When Max reads, it is like Jack can see the whole world of the book in his mind.

When the bell goes,
they are halfway through
the chapter. Max stands
up. "Gotta go," he says.
"Sorry. My friends will
be waiting for me on
the playground. Good to
meet you, though!"

"Yeah," says Jack. "Good
to meet you, too."

Jack feels **sad**. He wishes Max could keep reading to him forever.

"I'll tell you what," says Max. "Do you want to keep my book till tomorrow? That way, your mom or dad can read some more to you tonight."

Jack **gasps** as Max hands him the book.

He doesn't know what to say! Is Max really trusting him with his favorite book?

"Don't lose it, though!" Max jokes.

"I won't!" Jack promises. "Cross my heart!"

He looks down at his book buddy's copy of *Harry Potter*. It is **very old** and falling apart. Jack holds it like it is made of gold.

Chapter Five

When the bell goes,
Billie and Jamila have
only read three books.
Billie stands up and
stretches. Teaching
someone to read is tiring.

"Good work, girls,"
Mr. Parker says. He tells
Billie, "That is the most
books Jamila has ever
read!"

"Really?" says Billie. "Wow." She looks at Jamila. Jamila smiles up at her and she feels **warm** and **fuzzy** inside. She looks so proud.

"Four books tomorrow, Jamila?" Billie asks.

"You bet!" says Jamila happily.

Jamila runs to join her friends in the play corner.

"You don't have to come tomorrow," Mr. Parker says. "It was very kind of you to come today."

Billie shrugs. "That's all right," she says. "Jamila's my book buddy! I'm **happy** to help her."

The time has gone so quickly. Billie even forgot about the Reading Challenge.

Billie jogs back to her classroom to find Jack.

He is waiting for her by the door. When he sees Billie, he grins. "Look what I have!" he says.

Billie looks at the book Jack is holding. It's *Harry Potter*!

"What are you doing with that?" Billie says.

"You can't read that book! Even *I* can't read it yet. And I'm a **good** reader!"

"Maybe *I* can't read it," Jack says, smiling. "But my book buddy can!"

"When did you meet your buddy?" Billie asks Jack. She can't believe it!

"I thought you were hiding from him in the nurse's office?"

"I was!" Jack says. "But my book buddy came to find me. And he brought his copy of *Harry Potter* to read to me. How nice is that?"

"**Wow!**" says Billie. "That's *so* nice!"

"He's the best," says Jack. He tucks Max's book into his schoolbag. He feels so **lucky** to have such a cool and friendly book buddy. "How about you?" he asks. "Did you have a boring time with your buddy?"

"Nah," Billie says, smiling.

"She's fun actually. I think she really likes me, too! I like helping her to read."

Just then, Ms. Walton comes out of the classroom. "Jack! Billie!" she says. "How did you do with your book buddies? Did you read many books?"

Jack and Billie look at each other and **giggle**.

"Not really," says Billie. "We only read three."

"We didn't even finish one book!" says Jack, grinning.

"Oh dear," Ms. Walton says. "Do you want me to change your buddies?"

"No way!" Billie and Jack say together. Then they laugh.

"Sometimes there are more important things than winning, Ms. Walton," Billie reminds her teacher.

"Like making new friends!" says Jack.

Billie agrees. Then she takes Jack's hand and they run out into the sunshine.

About Sally Rippin

Sally Rippin was born in Darwin, Australia, and grew up in Southeast Asia. Sally is the author of many books for children, including the best-selling and beloved *Billie B. Brown*, *Hey Jack!* and *Polly and Buster* series. She lives in Melbourne with a naughty puppy and a delightful teenager, and writes and illustrates full-time.

Q&A with Sally!

What do you love most about Billie?

I love that Billie is brave. She is always happy to try new experiences. She is also happy to admit when she has done the wrong thing and to do her best to make it better.

What do you love most about Jack?

I love that Jack is kind. He is a good friend to Billie. Sometimes, being a good friend means telling the truth about how he feels, even if this is a hard thing to do.

Why do you think Billie and Jack are best friends?

Billie and Jack are a perfect match because they balance each other out. Billie is brave, but sometimes she does silly things. Jack is kind, but sometimes he is afraid to try new experiences. Together, they can take on the world!

What do you love most about your job?

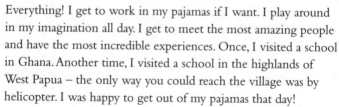

Everything! I get to work in my pajamas if I want. I play around in my imagination all day. I get to meet the most amazing people and have the most incredible experiences. Once, I visited a school in Ghana. Another time, I visited a school in the highlands of West Papua – the only way you could reach the village was by helicopter. I was happy to get out of my pajamas that day!

About Aki Fukuoka

Aki Fukuoka was born in Nagano, Japan. She now lives in Auckland, New Zealand, with her beautiful family. Aki has illustrated over 80 books. Her art has also been printed in magazines and on T-shirts, stationery, posters and murals.

Q&A with Aki!

What do you love most about Billie?

Billie is not afraid to speak her mind. She follows her heart when she is faced with a difficult situation. Also, I love her clothes!

What do you love most about Jack?

He is very kind and loyal. He tends to be shy and is quieter than Billie, but he always supports her and has her back!

If you could tell Billie one thing, what would it be?

You remind me of the friends that I admired throughout my school days. I was always a very shy and quiet girl and naturally gravitated towards confident girls with gleaming, bubbly personalities!

If you could tell Jack one thing, what would it be?

I would be happy if one of my boys grew up to be like you. Jack guides and supports Billie in his gentle yet grounded ways. Jack shows many strong attributes, without being aggressive or dominant. His parents must be so proud of him!

Billie's Favorite Books

Where the Wild Things Are
by Maurice Sendak

The Magic Finger
by Roald Dahl

I Just Ate My Friend
by Heidi McKinnon

The Hairy Maclary series
by Lynley Dodd

Diary of a Wombat
by Jackie French

Jack's Favorite Books

Would You Rather Be a Bullfrog?

by Dr. Seuss

Max

by Bob Graham

Old Tom

by Leigh Hobbs

The Tashi series

by Anna Fienberg

Magic Beach

by Alison Lester

Billie B. Brown

The Bad Butterfly

By Sally Rippin

Billie B. Brown

The Soccer Star

By Sally Rippin

Billie B. Brown

The Midnight Feast

By Sally Rippin

Billie B. Brown

The Second-best Friend

Billie B. Brown

The Extra-special Helper

By Sally Rippin

Billie B. Brown

The Beautiful Haircut

By Sally Rippin

Billie B. Brown

The Big Sister

Billie B. Brown

The Spotty Vacation

By Sally Rippin

Billie B. Brown

The Birthday Mix-up

By Sally Rippin

Billie B. Brown

The Secret Message

Billie B. Brown

The Little Lie

By Sally Rippin

Billie B. Brown

The Best Project

By Sally Rippin

Billie B. Brown

The Deep End

By Sally Rippin

Billie B. Brown

The Copycat Kid

By Sally Rippin

Billie B. Brown

The Night Fright

By Sally Rippin

Billie B. Brown

The Missing Tooth

By Sally Rippin

Billie B. Brown

The Bully Buster

By Sally Rippin

Which is your favorite?

Billie B. Brown & Hey Jack!

The Book Buddies

By Sally Rippin

Hey Jack! The Crazy Cousins By Sally Rippin

Hey Jack! The Scary Solo By Sally Rippin

Hey Jack! The Winning Goal By Sally Rippin

Hey Jack! The Robot Blues By Sally Rippin

Hey Jack! The Worry Monsters By Sally Rippin

Hey Jack! The New Friend By Sally Rippin

Hey Jack! The Worst Sleepover By Sally Rippin

Hey Jack! The Circus Lesson By Sally Rippin

Hey Jack! The Bumpy Ride By Sally Rippin

Hey Jack! The Top Team By Sally Rippin

Hey Jack! The Playground Problem By Sally Rippin

Hey Jack! The Best Party Ever By Sally Rippin

Hey Jack! The Bravest Kid By Sally Rippin

Hey Jack! The Big Adventure By Sally Rippin

Hey Jack! The Toy Sale By Sally Rippin

Hey Jack! The Star of the Week By Sally Rippin

Hey Jack! The Extra-special Group By Sally Rippin

Which is your favorite?

Billie B Brown & Hey Jack! The Book Buddies By Sally Rippin

My
Favorite Books